America
Raids
Britain

Robin Campbell

Published by

MELROSE BOOKS

An Imprint of Melrose Press Limited
St Thomas Place, Ely
Cambridgeshire
CB7 4GG, UK
www.melrosebooks.co.uk

FIRST EDITION

ISBN 978-1-909757-45-5

Printed and bound in Great Britain by:
Berforts Information Press, 23-25 Gunnels Wood Park,
Gunnels Wood Road, Stevenage, Hertfordshire, SG1 2BH

CONTENTS

CHAPTER 1

PREPARING TO SAIL

It was all noise, bustle, and hard work for the crew. The USS *Ranger* in April 1778 was being made ready for sea. At last the men on board the sloop-of-war sensed a change. It felt that they would soon be riding the waves again. They had been stationary for some weeks and had spent more time walking in the town than sailing the seas.

Of course the time spent in the French port of Nantes had been interesting. The different culture, the food, and the lively streets next to the harbour were all fascinating. However, this was not what they had crossed the Atlantic Ocean to do. Jake Smith, just like the other crew members, had the left the comfort of home to sail with Captain John Paul Jones. They wanted to fight for the USA, their newly constituted country. Sailing to meet and fight the foe was how that would be achieved, not resting in port.

Jake was one of the young midshipmen of the USS *Ranger*. He was just like the other midshipmen, feeling that he needed to show the crew, each day, that he knew what to do on board. He also had to make sure that Lieutenant Thomas Simpson, the officer who Captain Jones frequently turned to, saw that he knew what to do and when to do it.

Thomas Simpson was the officer who Captain Jones had known for longer than any other. He was among the first to be recruited to the *Ranger*, and he contributed to many of the earliest arrangements that were made for the voyage. It was no surprise therefore, that Captain Jones often seemed to use the suggestions made by Thomas.

It was fortunate for Jake that he knew what to do and could demonstrate that to be the case. His father had ensured that Jake was ready to sail in a larger ship. Together Jake and his father had sailed around the coves of Massachusetts on numerous occasions. From Rockport in the north, and south to Plymouth, they had spent many enjoyable days at sea. They had visited Boston and sailed in their small but well kept fishing boat among the larger boats that were anchored in the harbour.

Those visits to east coast ports in America only came after Jake had been taught about sailing and fishing nearer to home. And that he demonstrated that he had learnt what had been taught.

'Watch how I do it,' his father had often said.

Then, 'Do you think you can do that?'

'Make sure you get that knot tight, check it out now.'

Jake watched, tried, and often had to try again. Yet he did succeed eventually, although eventually was often not good enough for his father.

'You have to get it right first time,' his father reminded him. 'Try again.'

It was never enough to get it right at a second or third attempt. Jake had to get it right the first time and then every time, during what might be a long day at sea. It was hard for Jake and initially he had hated his father's insistence for perfection. However, as time passed he became better at preparing the boat and then sailing and fishing. The fishing, especially for cod, was hard work that also required skilful sailing. On occasions, strong winds, drenching rain, and an angry swell had caught them out when they were too far from the coast. Then Jake and his father had to work hard to reach land. Inevitably they had to work in unison, with Jake increasingly able to provide real support to the task. Sometimes the weather was dramatically different. Then it could be a mist or even a dense fog that suddenly descended on the boat. Jake and his father had to carefully and slowly head for the shore. All the time they had to listen out for any sound of the water lapping against the rocky coast, that might be dangerous.

With all that experience Jake was sure that he could perform every request made of him on board the *Ranger*. Now he was glad that his dad had been such an insistent and good teacher and that he had experienced so much sailing. It meant that the crew accepted him as a sailor. They were confident that this midshipman knew what he was doing and they saw evidence of this daily.

Now Jake and other members of the crew were getting the *Ranger* ready to sail again. The sails, ropes, and decks all had to be checked, repaired if necessary, and then checked again. They also modified masts in some instances, making them shorter. Then some masts were moved back from the bow by a few centimetres, all to make the *Ranger* faster and more manoeuvrable. There were also the guns as well as pistols and cutlasses to be cleaned and made ready. There was a variety of cannon shot that was brought on board including those such as star shot, that was several metal rods linked at one end by a metal hoop. When fired it opened out into a spinning star shape. Star shot would tear at sails and damage masts when fired at close range.

Everything being brought on board had to be just right. The officers made sure that was the case.

'Have you checked the ropes?' they asked of the midshipmen.

Of course the midshipmen had checked and rechecked the ropes.

'Are the guns ready for battle?'

Those too had been checked on numerous occasions.

So the answer was always clear and simple. 'Yes Sir.'

They dared not be found wanting when it came to preparations on board. For Jake the insistence of his father for perfection when sailing meant that everything had to be just right. It meant that checking and rechecking had become second nature to him. Whether at home in Massachusetts or at a port in France, Jake tried to be perfect in the preparations to sail.

The time in the safety of the harbour at Nantes had been productive in many ways. France was an ally of the USA during the War of Independence. So John Paul Jones was able to visit Benjamin Franklin, the American representative in Paris, and together they had planned the future voyage, as well as arranging for repairs to the sloop and provisions for the journey that lay ahead.

The time in Nantes had also meant that the men could relax and eat fresh food daily as well as drinking the local wines from the valley of the River Loire. They dare not think of the stale food and dried biscuits they would inevitably moan about after a very few days at sea, but the food they would have at sea was not yet uppermost in their minds. Getting the sloop in perfect condition for the journey ahead was what filled their time and their thoughts. There might also be handsome rewards to be gained if they could have a few victories at sea. They dreamed of such possibilities.

The USS *Ranger* had been made ready. All the wooden structure and sails were checked; repaired where necessary, and equipped for sea. Then the ships guns were prepared for battle. Finally the pistols and cutlasses that the men might use individually were cleaned, oiled, and checked daily. The USS *Ranger* was ready. There was just one final task before setting sail: to camouflage the sloop. A dull coloured cloth was used to cover as much of the hull as possible. When the USS *Ranger* set sail it did so disguised as a merchant ship.

As they left the confines of the town and headed out towards sea they passed a French squadron returning to the port. John Paul Jones immediately commanded that the stars and stripes be raised. Then he gave the order for a 13-gun salute. The French responded to that with their own gun salute. That response was really important and exciting. It meant that the stars and stripes of America had been given a formal military recognition. The cheers from the

USS *Ranger* resonated across the River Loire. Jake roared with the loudest of the crew. The excitement was evident among all on board. Jake noticed too that Captain Jones had a wide smile as he welcomed the honour given to the USS *Ranger* and to their nation of the United States of America.

Chapter 2
Travelling North

The crew had plenty to do as they departed the calm of the gentle River Loire and then the French shore. Away from the river and the coast the conditions were quite different. The Atlantic Ocean was wild. A strong wind was blowing. The waves were huge, dark, and menacing. Occasionally a larger wave would crash on to the deck of the *Ranger*, leaving behind a swirling river. As the sloop rose up and then down in the ocean that river rapidly disappeared overboard.

The sailors had wished to get away from land and again to sail the seas. That wish had been granted. It was now all hands on deck, lowering sails, tightening knots, and ensuring that all was secured.

Jake had experienced wild weather like this off the coast of Massachusetts, Maine and even as far north as Newfoundland, where the fishing for cod could be so productive. At times he and his father had to deal with very difficult conditions. Now here too near France there were problems. The strong wind was blowing straight at the small craft. At times any command from an officer could be lost in the wind. Then Jake and the other junior officers had to use their understanding of the sea and sailing to interpret the demands. The whole crew had wanted to get back to sea. Now the gale was giving them a demanding welcome on their return to the Atlantic Ocean.

'It's wild,' shouted Jake to a fellow midshipman as they worked together with rope and sail. The first call was swept aside by the howling wind.

'It's wild,' repeated Jake.

'It is and frightening,' came the reply.

Jake looked back to Samuel, his fellow junior officer. It was frightening but few sailors would admit it.

Jake nodded an agreement but added a more positive, 'We're doing well.'

'Do you think so?'

'No doubt about it, Samuel.' Jake looked across at him again; he seemed to be managing well even though his remarks did not suggest a great deal of confidence. Then Jake concentrated on his task.

With each monster wave the deck of the *Ranger* was given a thorough soaking. Then the sloop descended into the trough of the wave before rising again to receive yet more water across the deck. Moving about the boat was dangerous and each sailor gripped the safety ropes to keep standing. Jake could hardly believe the change from the quiet days in Nantes to the wild days at sea.

During a brief moment when Jake had been sent below deck, the order had been given to head back towards France. Now running with the wind the sloop was steadier in the water and the crew were relieved to be heading towards port. This time it was Brest that was their destination. It was a weary crew that eventually tied up the *Ranger*. The port in Brittany, north-west France, was not where they expected to be. All the crew had been looking forward to sailing again. Now they were all subdued, tired, soaked through, and glad to be back in a port

So as they had been battered there was a need to repeat all the checks on the equipment again. However, this time it was a very short stop for some running repairs. The *Ranger* also lost four crew who had been infected with smallpox and had to be left behind in Brest. Captain Jones had to hope that no other crew had contracted the disease. By April 10th they departed France for a second time. On this occasion conditions were much improved. So for the next 12 days events were quite different. There were to be numerous sightings of enemy vessels before they finally reached their destination in England.

'Sail ahead,' was the call from the deck alerting the crew that the real part of their journey was about to begin. The USS *Ranger* was north of the Scilly Isles, with England to the east on the starboard side of the sloop.

'All hands on deck.'

Then came the command of 'full sails.' The sloop creaked as it built up speed. The Dutch cargo boat in front of them floundered slowly and was rapidly caught. It gave no resistance as it was overwhelmed by the speed of the sloop and threatened by the weaponry on the American vessel.

'Get ready to board the merchant ship,' was the

command.

The task of securing the Dutchman, putting on board a small crew from the *Ranger* and then sending it on its way back to France was considered. However the cargo of flaxseed was not very valuable and the Dutch brigantine *Dolphin* would not fetch much of a price. So reluctantly, but sensibly the small *Dolphin* crew were transferred to the *Ranger* and their boat was scuttled.

Samuel smiled across to Jake, 'We did well.'

'We did Samuel. We did.' Jake was glad to hear a more positive comment after the turmoil of sailing against the gale.

'We'll achieve more victories before this trip is over,' Jake added with an authority that he did not yet possess.

As the USS *Ranger* sailed across the Irish Sea it met with other craft. A revenue cutter, which would normally pull alongside ships to determine if the cargo was legal, soon realised that it would be unwise to attempt this move on the *Ranger*. However, as it made its escape the sails were peppered with shots from the American guns. It might not be good news that the cutter was able to escape. Almost certainly reports of the presence of the boat would be known within days.

Shortly afterwards the *Lord Chatham* laden down with cargo was detected and stopped. This time the boat and the cargo were far more valuable. It included the baggage of a senior British Army officer, General Irwin, with the dining cutlery and plate alone being worth a few thousand pounds. So on this occasion a small crew led by John Seward boarded to sail the *Lord Chatham* back to Brest.

As the *Lord Chatham* sailed away from them a loud cheer went up from the crew on the *Ranger*. All the crew would share in the money raised from this capture. They had every reason to cheer. It was from the crew of that boat that John Paul learnt that the man-of-war *Drake* from England was in a nearby Irish port.

Although other minor skirmishes occurred, they were perhaps inevitable as the sloop sailed between England, Scotland, and Ireland. The Irish Sea was very busy and even on their short journey ships of various sizes and purpose were met. Those included a more sustained involvement with a Customs' boat, the *Hussar*. However, Captain Gurley had the more manoeuvrable of the boats and was able to out run the *Ranger* and head for what he considered to be safety in the port of Whitehaven.

Before continuing with his intended raid upon that port, Captain John Paul Jones was determined to assess the *Drake* and the possibility of defeating it. The USS *Ranger* entered the Irish harbour. Again their sloop-of-war gave the appearance of being a merchant ship. The setting sun helped in the disguise and as the *Ranger* directly approached the *Drake* and answered that boat's calls and whistles nothing appeared to be amiss. John Paul was even able to bring the *Ranger* alongside the *Drake* so that all available guns were aimed at the British boat.

The men on board were absolutely silent. They were ready to attack the *Drake* if ordered to do so. Then just as the perfect plan was about to be executed a strong squall rushed through the harbour. The winds had again influenced the *Ranger*. Now it was all hands on deck, attention to the sails and an inevitable move away from the *Drake*. John Paul took the quick decision to manoeuvre the sloop back out into the

Irish Sea.

'All hands to the deck.'

'Sails.'

Incredibly the short commands seemed to be adequate. Everyone on board seemed to be aware instantly of what was required of them.

'Steady lads.'

Captain John Paul Jones was both pleased and disappointed. Pleased to have got close to the *Drake* without being detected, disappointed to have to back off because of the weather. Many of the sailors were quietly pleased, rather than disappointed. A battle with a large man-of-war had been averted, at least for the moment.

Once out in the Irish Sea, Captain John Paul Jones realised it was time to move towards the main target. The adventures at sea and the victories against smaller craft were bonuses. It was time to make an audacious attack on an English port.

CHAPTER 3
HEADING FOR WHITEHAVEN

Looking eastwards towards the English coast John Paul Jones could not yet see the outline of Whitehaven. The hills and mountains inland could perhaps be picked out in the partial darkness of a late spring night. In particular John Paul thought that the mountain of Skiddaw in the northern Lake District and the Scafell range to the south could be seen. Although how much of that sighting might have been based on a prior knowledge of what existed rather than a true sighting, at that moment was difficult to determine. John Paul Jones was now a captain in the US Navy but he had learnt about sailing in this very town. Whitehaven was where he had been apprenticed to Captain Benson when he was just 13 years old.

He was born in Scotland and he had travelled south to the important port of Whitehaven to begin an apprenticeship in seamanship. Now, however, he was an American and it was his knowledge of Whitehaven, albeit a somewhat limited knowledge from childhood, that suggested that this port would be a good target. When he had first arrived at Whitehaven as a youngster from Scotland it was for just a short stay before sailing to Virginia and Barbados in the *Friendship*. He returned to the port in England a number of times but each stay was typically brief, before he set sail again. He sailed in a number of different ships after the owners of his first boat had financial problems and he was released from his apprenticeship after four years.

Now, in 1778, he had returned to Whitehaven, but for a very different purpose. He hoped to inflict revenge on England for the frequent Royal Navy raids on east coast American towns. John Paul thought they might be able to do some damage to the trade that left daily into the Irish Sea as well as that which arrived from various countries around the world. Whatever they could achieve would constitute a rude awakening to the Royal Navy and the supposed invincibility of England as a country.

John Paul Jones had in his mind what might be

possible and how to go about achieving that. As he looked towards Whitehaven he ran through those plans in his mind again. However, from time-to-time his thoughts, perhaps inevitably, drifted as he recalled his brief stay in that town and his childhood.

It had been a wrench to leave his home town of Kirkbean in Scotland and to head south. John Paul recalled the hills, the sea, and the work of his father as gardener on the Arbigland Estate. It was the simple two-roomed cottage on the estate where he had been born on July 6th 1747.

The Arbigland Estate, Kirkbean School, and the port of Carsethorn were his world until the age of 13. Those three sites formed most of the area that was home to John Paul during those early years. The Arbigland Estate was the most southerly of the three on the banks of the River Nith where it joined the Solway Estuary. Kirkbean lay to the north but just over a mile from home and also about a mile from the river. Carsethorn on the river was further north from the cottage where John Paul lived. Yet in some sense it was the centre of his childhood.

It was a childhood of freedom and adventure, but

also of hard work helping his father on the estate. Away from that work and school his adventures frequently took him in one direction; that was to the port where somehow a love of the sea was developed even before he spent any great time sailing.

John Paul and his friend William might come out of the school together but that was often short lived.

'I'm away,' John Paul would call out as he ran down the slope from Kirkbean School towards the port of Carsethorn on the River Nith and the Solway Firth. The River Nith came from the north and the town of Dumfries; the Solway flowed from the east and out to the Irish Sea.

'I'll follow you down, John,' was the typical reply from William.

William was content to follow walking and occasionally breaking into a slow run. He had more time to enjoy the sights of the hills, the rivers and the port.

'I'll be at the port,' John added as he gathered speed on the downhill slopes.

William smiled as he heard that comment.

'I'll see you there,' William shouted as a reply.

Of course John would be at the port. John was always at the port. He was there at every possible opportunity. He talked to the sailors, asked questions about the ships and where they were bound. The teacher at Kirkbean would have found it difficult to recognise the inquisitive and constantly questioning young boy. This was not the lad who sat daydreaming and quiet in the classroom every day. Yet John Paul was learning as much, even more perhaps, out of doors among the boats at the port.

Given the opportunity John would clamber all over a boat. He would examine ropes, clamber over the deck, and question, question, question any sailor or officer who was prepared to give him some time. Not that all the crew he met were interested in talking to him. Some quite clearly saw him as a nuisance and were quick to send him away from the boat. Then John Paul would have to move along the riverbank to find another crew willing to give him some time, perhaps even getting him to complete a few tasks on board. From those visits, conversations, and tasks he was becoming a knowledgeable sailor before he ever set sail. An understanding of sailing developed week by week. And there was plenty of time for John Paul to dream about the sea while at school.

Carsethorn, or plain Carse as it was sometimes known was quite busy as a port for trade in the Solway Estuary. It also maintained a flourishing trade with Ireland and the Isle of Man. So there was almost inevitably sailing craft and cargo boats for John Paul to see and hopefully explore. It was only in later years that the Carse became a port of departure for emigration by thousands to North America, Australia, and New Zealand in the late 1700s and early 1800s.

Just occasionally as they left school William might be able to convince John Paul to explore inland. In particular Criffel stood at 1,867 feet above sea level. From the peak of that hill, or mountain, views of the rivers and sea could provide a magnet for William to use to vary the activities.

'Let's climb Criffel today, John,' William tried as an opening on leaving school.

'What about the Carse?' was the reply from John Paul.

'You're right John. The view of Carse and the rivers will be grand today, we'll be able to count the ships and decide where they are going to or coming from.' William chose his words with great care to talk about the Carse at the same time suggesting a different destination and objective for their outing

John Paul looked intently at William then started on the uphill walk. The sea could be enjoyed from a distance as well as close up, especially on a clear day. There were other days when the mountain was covered in a shroud of cloud. On those cloudy days there were occasions when Criffel might not be visible at all from the port. But on a bright day on the mountain John did enjoy the views of the Carse from Criffel. He could see the port and ships laid out like models of the real ships. He could dream of where those ships might take him in the future. Those dreams were now turning into a reality. It was a reality beyond any of the thoughts he had as a child.

Chapter 4
Close by Whitehaven

On board the USS *Ranger* the sailors and marines were prepared to go ashore. This was the one of the more difficult parts of the sequence. Ready to go and getting more nervous about the outcome with nothing left to do except wait. They had checked their pistols and cutlasses then checked them again. Wait, check, and wait. It made for a nervous crew.

Jake Smith felt a shiver down his spine.

'It's a cold night,' he thought to himself.

But it was a bit more than just the cold that made him shiver. As Midshipman Smith looked across the sea separating the USS *Ranger* from the small town on the horizon he feared the possible outcome. It was not just the French spring in Nantes that had given warmth to the air that was now missing. Now it was really the thought of what was to come that made him feel cold. Here the USS *Ranger* was at most two miles from the town of Whitehaven on the west coast of northern England. It was late at night, almost midnight, on April 22nd 1778 and as it was a clear night it was cold and frosty at this time of year.

Jake pulled his jacket tighter round his chest as though that might get rid of his shivers. As he looked towards the shoreline he could only detect the outline of the fort guarding the harbour, the rest of the town could only be imagined. The large guns that served as protection for the harbour and the town were too far in the distance to be recognised. Nevertheless he imagined there would be 32-pound cannons ready to blast the long boats in any attempt to enter the harbour and perhaps even more so for their return. Their safety might all depend on how vigilant the guards were, how quickly the boats could be manoeuvred, how quietly the rocks and wall of the harbour could be climbed and how dark it remained.

Only hours earlier, the attempt to land to the south of the town had been unsuccessful. The rocky coastline had made landing difficult and with a rough sea the plan had been foiled. That failure had led to mutterings from some of the crew, especially perhaps from those who had been soaked by the cold sea. They were more content when sailing the seas, as recent events had shown. Dangerous landings and fights on shore might suit the marines but it was not what the men expected. Most of the crew were sailors and the sea was their home. Aware of this discontent, the officers were talking quietly but firmly to some of the more vocal members of the crew.

Midshipman Jake Smith had not expected that any officer would speak to him. After all he had not voiced any discontent and he was more concerned with completing all his duties as requested.

'Nothing to worry about tonight,' said a voice behind him.

Jake turned and was astonished to see the Captain John Paul Jones, standing just behind him.

'No, sir,' replied Jake bringing himself to attention. 'I was just wondering how things might work out,' he added.

'We will be fine. Just do what is asked of you and it will be a success,' stated the Captain.

'Yes, sir,' was as much as Jake could manage as a reply.

Jake stood ramrod straight as he was addressed by his much-admired Captain. The desire to be well thought of was important to any midshipman. Jake Smith was no exception to that rule. John Paul Jones paused for a moment as though to add something to their brief talk but then instead moved past Jake and continued along the short deck of this sloop-of-war. Jake watched as the Captain stopped to talk briefly with another one of the crew before moving on around the deck. Although John Paul Jones was not tall he seemed to dominate anyone he was talking to by his very presence. All the crew were in awe of their famous captain. Their fears for the outcome of the daring invasion were lessened by his words of encouragement.

Jake's spirits had been lifted by the short contact and conversation with the Captain. To be spoken to in such a friendly way was an honour. Yet Jake knew that he would still have to do well on the expedition. The expectation was that all the crew would perform their allotted tasks bravely and without hesitation.

'I think I can do it,' Jake said to himself.

He did not want to show any sign of fear to those around him. So he continued to stand, almost at full attention gazing out to their objective.

'I will do it,' Jake assured himself.

From the 140 officers and enlisted men only a carefully selected crew of 30 would be rowing to the shore. For a group of powerful sailors it was regarded as a short distance to the harbour. Nevertheless there would almost a mile or more of open sea to be rowed. Jake was one of the selected crew. He was in the boat with the Captain together with the second-in-command the Swedish Lieutenant Meijer. The second boat was commanded by one of the US marines Lieutenant Samuel Wallingford while Midshipman Ben Hill had the important second-in-command role.

Each of the raiding party had a pistol and a cutlass with which to do battle. Jake felt the handle of his pistol. It made him feel brave and adult, but it also had the opposite effect and made him just a bit frightened. The many possible outcomes swirled around in his head. He was a good shot with a gun, he reminded himself. When he was at home in Massachusetts shooting at wildlife to provide food for the table, he was frequently successful. Aiming at another person, with the intent to harm, might be quite different, thought Jake.

Jake looked across at his friend Samuel who seemed to be very relaxed. The tension that was apparent in many was not evident in Samuel.

'If Samuel can do it, so can I,' Jake told himself. Now he began to feel more relaxed.

'I will do it.' Jake was now truly ready for the attack.

Chapter 5
Rowing to the Harbour

'Lower away.' The command when it came was softly spoken but clear.

Immediately the tension of waiting seemed to be lifted. Now there was a buzz of activity. The boats were lowered gently into the water and as they touched the sea Jake's stomach tightened. He began to worry again that he might not live up to the expectation of being brave and making a positive contribution to the raid. Yet he knew that this test of his ability and courage had to be met full on and won. The negative thoughts and concerns were soon forgotten as he moved to the front of the boat.

At the bow Jake's important role was to keep an eye on the direction of the boat. He also had to check for any obstacle that might create problems. After the difficulties with rocks to the south of the town, the whole crew, not just Jake, were concerned. However, they all realised that in truth there was no reason for such worries. They were after all heading directly now for the harbour. Daily much bigger craft came in and out of the busy port. There were no obvious physical barriers to delay their safe journey into Whitehaven.

If there were to be any danger it would be related to the vigilance of the guards. If the two boats were recognised and the guards understood what might be occurring then they could easily be blown out of the water. However, why should the guards expect an invasion or a raid from the sea? England had not been invaded for centuries. The task of being on guard did not include any thoughts of being attacked from the sea. On the American east coast the population of towns and seaports had constantly to be watching for attacks from the British ships. There it was a daily threat and a real problem for the whole community. That was not the case in ports around the northern English coast.

'Push off,' came the command.

The boat carrying Captain John Paul Jones led the departure from the mother ship. Immediately the burly and strong sailors pulled on their oars and took the boats clear of the USS *Ranger*.

As the boats rose and fell across the waves Jake Smith could catch a limited view of the harbour through the darkness of the night as the boat rode the crest of a wave. Then it all disappeared as the boat dipped and faced down into the waves. During these initial strokes Lieutenant Meijer called out from time-to-time from the stern to encourage and guide the crew. The second craft was a small distance behind but maintaining the same speed as the lead vessel. Occasionally Jake spotted it out of the corner of his eye on his left hand, or port side.

In the other boat Lieutenant Wallingford was also giving instructions from the stern. However, in addition he had the task of controlling the speed and direction so that he remained just behind and to the side of the Captain's boat. He needed to remain in visual contact with that boat. Yet, he also needed to keep a short distance away from it so that if they were sighted and became a target for the large fort guns their closeness did not create an easy target. Like Jake, Midshipman Ben Hill was positioned at the front of the small craft. Additionally, he had the task of signalling back details to ensure that the speed and direction of the boat was in tune with the leading craft.

Although some of the sailors might have moaned earlier about going on land to fight, the hard rowing was part of what they accepted. It was a strenuous row against the tide. So instead of being a relative short journey it would take close to three hours to cover the distance from the USS *Ranger* to the harbour.

'What can you see?' asked Lieutenant Meijer quietly. His voice just reached Jake as the men splashed their oars and the small boat creaked.

'Clear ahead,' replied Jake.

'No signs of activity by the fort,' he added.

'Well, keep your eyes peeled,' came the softly spoken instruction from the lieutenant.

'Yes sir,' whispered Jake. He needed to get his reply to the lieutenant but not create too much noise. Still the harbour showed no sign of activity.

John Paul Jones just kept on looking ahead and said nothing. The time for orders and activity was fast approaching.

Meanwhile the most obvious change that was occurring was a small glimmer of light beginning to appear on the horizon as they approached from the west. The Captain reflected that a small amount of light would make their task easier. But getting light also increased the risk of being seen. Even as the Captain thought about the light the lead boat began move more smoothly through the water. They were beginning to get some protection from the harbour walls.

Captain Jones looked back towards Lieutenant Meijer. That was all that was needed. The Lieutenant started directing the boat towards the fort. The occupants of the first boat needed to ensure that both boats would be able to leave Whitehaven without a risk coming from the guns. The tension was now rising again as the boat closed in by the wall of the harbour entrance.

'Quietly lads,' he whispered.

The sailors were quiet but every sound made them think they would be overheard. At the bow Jake raised his right hand to indicate that they were nearing their landing point.

'Almost there,' added the Captain.

They were nearly ready for action. Although for

the Lieutenant his action was to stay behind with a few men to guard their boat.

In the other boat Lieutenant Wallingford was heading in the opposite direction towards where the numerous ships anchored in the harbour.

'Steady,' he uttered softly.

Like the Captain, Samuel Wallingford wanted to escape detection until the last possible moment, or avoid it altogether. His marines were ready for what they expected would be a tough battle with the guards as well as the residents of the town. Then, and only after a battle, would they be able to complete their main task to set fire to the boats in the harbour. That would send a very loud message that America was fighting for its independence.

Chapter 6
Attacking the fort

Captain John Paul Jones was the first to land. As he jumped across to the harbour wall two sailors followed him within seconds. John Paul looked carefully at the possible short routes that might be taken. He didn't so much as glance at the activity behind him. He trusted his men to do the job that was required of them. In the meantime the sailors had turned the boat and secured and arranged it in a way that it could depart whenever required.

Within minutes John Paul had worked out a route over the harbour wall and on to the battlements. The men were instructed mainly by hand signals on the route to use. However, occasionally John Paul Jones gave a softly spoken instruction.

'Don't let your cutlass bang against the rocks.'

'You might need to use the shoulder of the person next to you as a foothold.'

'Keep together at the top.'

'Stay put on top until I give an instruction.'

'We'll all need to look out for the guards.'

At times it seemed as though there was always another instruction being transmitted from the Captain to the men. Yet somehow it was all completed very quietly.

Now for Lieutenant Meijer in the boat at the foot of the battlements there was nothing to see. All the men in raiding party were over the wall and out of sight. The Lieutenant's task of guarding the boat now seemed a lonely and unexciting part of the raid. There was one other sailor in the boat. However, he was at the front of the boat and any communication at this stage was by hand signals albeit in the half-light of morning. Before leaving the USS *Ranger* the Captain had emphasised the importance of his role.

'You are key to this operation lieutenant. You must have the boat ready to leave at any time,' the Captain spoke directly to Meijer.

'Yes sir,' he replied.

'Without you the whole exercise could be a failure,' added John Paul looking at Meijer with clear eye contact for emphasis.

At the harbour wall the Lieutenant recalled the conversation and remained extra vigilant.

'Quiet,' the Captain whispered as the sailors completed the climb and reached the battlement.

For a moment Jake thought the Captain must be concerned for the success of the attack. He seemed to be whispering 'Quiet' almost constantly. There was already a tense stillness in the air and complete silence. All of the men were quiet, thinking perhaps of the action to come. Jake considered that perhaps beyond the clear authority that the Captain demonstrated, there was a slight nervousness.

The Captain now moved again to the front and directed two of the sailors to remain at this point. Then he quietly moved forward to what appeared to be the guardhouse. At the same time he beckoned for the main group to follow him. Now Jake realised that either the fort was unguarded, or perhaps the guards had confidently retired for the night and were inside the guardhouse. After all, for them it was a settled and quiet life. Occasionally they might need to separate a couple of fighters who had perhaps drunk too much.

Then they were there to back up the officials at the port as cargo boats arrived and were unloaded. Repelling invaders had never been considered, indeed it was unthinkable that any would attack a British port.

Clearly, the news of an American sloop in the Irish Sea could not it seemed have reached this port or if news had arrived it was largely discounted.

The Captain and his men were now by the side of the sturdy gatehouse door. The heavy timber and metal studs gave it an appearance of being strong, thick, and not easily knocked in. Either side of the door there were large stone walls that were part of the construction of the solid building. However, John Paul Jones seemed confident that he was going to be able to gain access to the building. He beckoned to Jake.

'When I give the signal I need you to try opening the door.'

Flabbergasted, Jake hesitated then looked quizzically at the Captain.

'Sir?' Jake really could not understand what the Captain expected of him.

'I think we can just open the door with the handle.'

That sounded far too easy to Jake; but it was not his

role to question the authority of his Captain. So Jake replied with a repeated but more forceful 'Sir.' There was no hesitation or question in the spoken word the second time.

Jake started to move forward but the Captain restrained him. 'Leave your weapons to the side of the door. They will create too much noise as you open the door.'

'When you open the door, dive and roll to the side.'

'Your timing will be important.'

'Yes Sir,' said Jake.

'Whatever occurs when you open the door, you must very quickly get away from the entrance. We will then have a clear path to overwhelm whoever is inside. Once we are all past you then you pick up your pistol and cutlass from the side of the door and join us in the battle.'

Then turning to the crew John Paul added, 'We jump over or past the midshipman and see if we can overwhelm the guards.'

'Do you all understand?' he added, looking at each of the men in turn.

Jake could feel his heart thumping in his chest. It

had reached the point now where he just wanted to get started.

'Quietly lads,' whispered the Captain. He gave a final look round the scene then turned to face the door.

'Now!' the order was softly but firmly given.

Jake grasped the door handle. The cold of the metal handle made Jake pause, but then he applied pressure and pushed the handle down. He was surprised that the large handle moved so easily. Then using his shoulder Jake pushed at the door. It swung open much easier than could have been expected. As Jake shoved the door wide open and rolled to the side he felt the rush of sailors from behind him.

Once it was all clear Jake was up on his feet and then retrieved his weapons. He followed the last of the group through the doorway. Now they were all in the guardhouse and a noisy attacking force replaced the quiet. They were all ready for the battle; but it was a battle that didn't occur.

The guards were fast asleep!

Chapter 7
Spiking the guns

The sailors and marines in the raiding party were overjoyed to have captured the guardhouse with such ease. The bleary-eyed guards had very quickly been tied up and made secure within the building.

'What are you doing? Who are you?' the sergeant guard, who had been in charge, asked.

'You'll know shortly,' was the terse reply.

The guardhouse sergeant was confused. He couldn't work out what had happened. He was also very concerned that he and the other guards had been overwhelmed and made prisoner so easily. And they had all been asleep when attacked. That might not sound too good when the harbourmaster tried to establish what had taken place.

The sergeant looked at the various crew members but couldn't work out who they might be. They didn't have the look of pirates or privateers; but perhaps they were. The Captain in charge was well dressed and spoke with a Scottish accent, or so it seemed. Why had they attacked? The sergeant hoped that by listening in very carefully he would get some idea of what had happened.

'Well done men, you all did very well,' indicated John Paul Jones.

Jake was proud of what had been achieved. However, the more he thought about it the less difficult it seemed. What had Jake done? He had opened a large heavy door. That was it!

He had really thought he would have to do a lot more than open a door! Even as he had followed the sailors into the depths of the guardhouse he was merely in time to see the guards being tied up. No shots, no injuries, no fighting: it had been a strange landing and attack.

Still, in a way Jake was glad that it had all been so easy. His nervous anxiety from before the attack was gone. Nevertheless at the back of his mind was the thought that the raid was far from over. John Paul Jones soon indicated that what he saw as the important part of the attack on this side of the harbour had yet to occur.

'We need to spike the guns,' he stated. The guardhouse sergeant worked out why even before the Captain gave details. With the guns spiked the raiders would be able to escape without any chance of being shot at with the large 32-pounders. Those guns, if left in working order, would be able to reach a mile from shore. That would not happen if they had been spiked. Then they would be unusable.

John Paul Jones gave the spike bag to Jake and signalled to the other midshipman, Joe Green to join them. Quickly they strode out of the guardhouse. At the first gun he indicated how they would proceed.

'We'll need a spike for each gun,' he stated, looking at Jake. To Joe he added, 'You'll give the hammer to me at each gun. We will have to work quickly because we are bound to be noisy.'

Jake was ready with the first spike that he held out for the Captain. Joe followed by having the hammer ready as well. John Paul placed the first spike in the touch hole for firing the gun. With a few sharp bangs he tapped the spike deep into gun. There was one less gun to worry about when they needed to leave the harbour. There would be little chance that any guard would be able to get the spikes out with any speed, if at all.

'You! I need you over here,' John Paul called out to one of the sailors. 'I want you to watch what I'm doing and tell me if you can do the job.'

The sailor watched one spike being hammered into the touch hole. 'Yes sir, ' he indicated. 'I can do that.'

'Take the hammer and show me you can.'

The sailor did as he was asked and demonstrated with the first blow on the next spike that he could do the job very well indeed. His powerful arms ensured that he could hammer the spikes home with ease. His rhythm of tap, tap, bang, tap, tap, ensured that each spike was well hammered into place.

They quickly moved on to the next gun and that too they spiked. The trio rapidly got into a rhythm that ensured each gun was spiked in a very short time. Jake and Joe were clearly excited that they were contributing so much to the attack on the harbour.

'Don't dawdle,' commanded the Captain. They were actually moving quite quickly and not wasting a moment as they spiked each gun in turn. It really was just a comment to keep the momentum going and to give John Paul a moment to exert his authority again.

'Well done, we're nearly finished,' that comment from the Captain more accurately indicated how well they had all done. Jake now felt a warm glow from the activity, as running with the bag of spikes from one gun to the next gave some internal heat. Jake was also excited and warmed, beyond the exercise, by what they had achieved

'Last one,' John Paul Jones stated as he supervised the final gun being spiked. Here the sailor seemed to give an extra hard bang on the spike as if to complete the task in style.

'Good. Let's get back to the guardhouse.'

The trio followed the Captain back towards the first gun. The Captain led them on the return but Joe was carrying the hammer and Jake the bag with a few remaining spikes, and the sailor was glancing at each spiked gun as they returned towards the guardhouse.

The sergeant of the guards had developed some idea of the attack. He had worked out that the ship had come directly from France. Also, that there had been some successful skirmishes in the Irish Sea. Incredibly he was also beginning to think that it was an American ship that was attacking the town. That was hard to accept but possibly true, he thought.

For different reasons each of the 'spikers' felt a tiredness in their arms. But none of them said a word about the effort that had been put into the task. The important fact was that if they could complete their attack on the port then they would be able to return to the *Ranger* in relative safety. It was unlikely that they could be bombarded by these 32-pounders.

John Paul Jones was less pleased when he noted that the sailors and marines in the second boat had not yet been able to put to fire any of the boats in the harbour.

Chapter 8
Capturing the Old Quay

Lieutenant Samuel Wallingford had led the second boat just behind and to the side of the leading boat. Then, as John Paul Jones landed and started to scale the battlements, Wallingford had changed direction carefully to head across the harbour to the Old Quay. It was there that the ships to be torched were anchored. Now it became even more important to keep quiet.

Lieutenant Wallingford was aware of the gentle lapping sound of the water in the harbour. It was a useful shield to any noise that their rowing might create. Looking over his shoulder and back to where John Paul had landed he was surprised by the lack of any sound coming from that attack party. Still if it meant that his group was going to remain undetected then all to the good.

Nevertheless, the paddles had to be lowered

carefully into the water for each stroke. Hitting the water with a force would send a well-known sound across the harbour. The residents, or crews of boats, might be alerted by such noise. However, the American crew were too well trained to allow a heavy hand to defeat their attack. The boat was gently rowed across the harbour. A soft pull on the oars, then a short rest as the boat was steered between the vessels anchored close together in the busy port. That was followed by another soft paddle. There was no need to say anything. Hand signals could very effectively inform the crew of what was required.

Just before reaching the Old Quay their soft, almost noiseless paddling, was interrupted by a tap, tap, bang, tap, tap noise from near to the guardhouse. The Lieutenant was pleased and annoyed to hear the sound. Pleased because it must mean that the guardhouse had been captured and the big guns were being spiked. Disappointed because the sound might be detected and an alarm would be raised if anyone worked out what was happening.

'Three quick strokes now lads,' was the quiet command given. That was all that was left to be done to reach the Old Quay.

'Store your oars,' was the next order.

The boat with the second raiding party was now hard up against the steps leading onto the quay.

Lieutenant Samuel Wallingford was now ready to lead his marines onto the quay and then to torch some of the ships in the harbour.

'Marines to the top of the stairs and ready to battle,' was the order given by the Lieutenant.

'Don't move beyond the stairs until I have had time to check the situation,' he added. Carefully he climbed the stairs and looked along the quay. There was no sign of anyone. There was now a pale light from the advancing dawn. Even so, there was no evidence of anyone stirring in the town. Although it seemed as though this might be a good opportunity to torch the boats, there was a problem. The candles that they brought from the USS *Ranger* had burnt out! They had no light of any kind to complete the task. On the other side of the harbour John Paul Jones was in a similar predicament. Although the Captain was annoyed that no boats in the harbour had been torched, he was nevertheless aware that the candles that his party had brought had gone out. He assumed with annoyance that the same had probably occurred in the other boat.

A solution was at hand. Captain John Paul ordered two of the sailors to obtain a torch from the guardhouse.

'Make sure there's plenty of burning left on the torch.'

The two sailors soon found some new torches ready to burn and were able to light them from torches already burning.

'New torches, sir.'

'Good, we'll head along the pier and give a hand to the other party,' replied the Captain. This reply was really an order.

In the guardhouse the tied-up guards wondered about the torches.

'It will be getting light now, surely,' stated one of the guards.

'Perhaps they have some other purpose for the torches,' replied the sergeant.

'What do you mean?'

'They might intend to torch a boat or two.'

'No, surely not. Why would they do that?' The confused guard asked.

'I think they're foreigners who want to do our trade some harm,' was the guess made by the sergeant.

'So where are they from? They didn't sound French, did they?'

'No, I think they might be American,' the sergeant suggested. 'I think they've gone round to the Old Quay now.'

'We need to try to get untied.'

On the other side of the harbour Lieutenant Wallingford indicated to his men that they would force an entry into the nearest house to get a light of some kind. A few of the men recognised that the nearest dwelling was a public house, and so became keen to attempt the attack.

'Right we'll go,' Samuel ordered.

Once they reached the house, entry was easy. The door was not fully secured. Inside it became obvious immediately that they were indeed inside a public house.

'I want everyone to be tied up. We will need two torches and you can all have a quick drink before we go.' The lieutenant had decided that to attempt to stop his crew from drinking would have been impossible. So ordering them to have a quick drink before departing seemed to be a good option. He noted that the drinking seemed to be the first task that was completed by the crew and he waited a moment before reminding them of the other part of the activity that was part of the order given.

By this time Nicholas Allison and his family were thoroughly roused and very displeased with what they saw happening. They were also confused because they didn't recognise any of the party.

'What do you think you are up to and who are you?'

Lieutenant Wallingford decided the time was ripe to make known what they were about.

'We are troops and sailors from the United States of America. We are here to show that we too can raid ports and disrupt trade.'

'But you won't get away with it.'

'I think we are doing just that,' he replied proudly.

'Right men, your last drink now. Let's get the torches outside to do what we came to do. That's an order. Go, go, go.'

All the men tumbled out of the public house. Some wobbled a bit more than others. However, they were all ready now to continue with the task of torching some boats.

Chapter 9
TORCHING THE BOATS

As Lieutenant Wallingford's men tumbled, or wobbled, out of the Inn they were aware of Captain Jones and his party coming around the pier to the Old Quay.

'Step lively lads,' exclaimed Lieutenant Wallingford.

'Captain Jones will be joining us soon.'

His comment had a sobering effect upon his party. None of the men would wish to do anything that might displease the Captain.

'Are you having trouble Lieutenant?' called John Paul from a distance.

'About to torch now Sir,' he called back, without answering the question about troubles.

Captain Jones had himself stopped his group to get another light from a house. He was aware that the same problem had probably occurred with the Lieutenant's lights. He decided to concentrate on what needed to be done rather than what had not happened. As he neared the Old Quay he questioned the Lieutenant.

'Which boat are you heading for first?' he asked.

'The large one near to the quay. The *Thompson*.'

'A good choice Lieutenant, well done.'

The *Thompson* was a new ship that had already been loaded and ready to sail to Dublin with the next tide. It was full of coal so it was an ideal target for the raiders. It was also anchored very close to the *Saltham* so that it might be possible to get two craft burning within a short space of time.

'Midshipman,' the Captain called, looking at Jake Smith as he did so. Jake immediately rushed forward. 'Join the raiding party to the boats.'

'Yes, sir,' said Jake as he reached the Captain.

More softly the Captain informed Jake, 'you can let me know about those two boats after they've been torched.'

'Sir.'

'And take this torch with you.'

Jake moved across the quay to join the other party, but he was aware that he might be regarded as an interloper by the marines and sailors of Lieutenant

Wallingford's group. He would have to be diplomatic in his dealings with each of the groups heading out to the *Thompson* and *Saltham*.

'Another torch from the Captain sir,' he sensibly stated as he stood before Lieutenant Wallingford.

'Good. We might need use of that when we board the two boats.'

'Follow me men, we'll get the bigger ship first.'

'Midshipman Hill take two men and check below deck to see if there are any sailors left on board as guards,' the Lieutenant ordered. 'If this ship is anything like everything else we've seen they will probably be asleep.' Then he added a cautionary, 'but check carefully and be alert.'

'Check every corner of below deck,' Ben Hill called to his small group of attackers.

'Over here sir,' called one of the two marines.

Midshipman Hill ducked his head and went forward to face the enemy. Instead he came upon three bleary-eyed young boys who had been woken from a deep sleep.

'What are you on board for?'

'We're... we're guarding the ship,' replied the

tallest lad hesitantly, looking down at his feet.

'You guard it with your eyes closed; do you?' said Hill.

'Once the town goes quiet we can get a bit of rest.'

Ben Hill looked at the trio. 'You can join us if you wish. We will make real sailors out of you.'

'I don't think we can do that sir,' replied the tall lad.

'You'll get good rewards with us lads. We share our spoils and you'll do well.'

Midshipman Hill paused briefly to see if they were going to join up, then stated, 'Alright then, take them up on deck and they come with us when we go back to the quay.'

'Can we get dressed sir?'

'No. If you are not joining us you might as well stay in your night shirts.'

Midshipman Hill turned to Jake and the marines. 'Gag them before we leave, we don't want them stirring up the town when we get back on land.'

The three youngsters were soon tied at the wrists and gagged to stop them raising a warning.

Back on the deck it had been a hive of activity. As the group emerged from below deck they witnessed a barrel of tar being scattered around the main mast. There were pieces of canvas and chunks of wood used for repairs being thrown in loose heaps on the deck. Wallingford's men were creating the basis for what they hoped would be an inferno.

Two other lads had been captured without any difficulty from the *Saltham* and they too were tied up. Each of the boys captured was shocked by what had happened. So too would be Captain Richard Johnson of the biggest ship the *Thompson*. This was the ship in greatest danger of being destroyed by fire. If that happened then other craft would be likely to destroyed too because the ships were very close together and at low tide they would not be able to escape from the harbour.

Samuel Wallingford felt it was time to torch the *Thompson*. They had been on board the boat for long enough and now they should leave Whitehaven as well. News of their attack on the port might have been spread around the town and more widely. It was time to go.

'Light the fire,' he ordered. A marine with a torch immediately set light to heaps of canvas and wood near the main mast. Within seconds the fire seemed to catch hold.

'Back on shore,' he called.

The marines and sailors were very willing to respond to that order. The morning was dawning and soon port workers and sailors would be arriving at the harbour for work. Then there was a real danger that the Americans would be greatly outnumbered.

Jake rushed to the Captain. 'The *Thompson* is well lit, sir.'

Captain Paul Jones was pleased with the news but now he too was getting impatient to leave. 'Back to the boats,' he called out.

The men responded with speed. Each of the Americans was very aware of the increasing danger with every minute that they remained in Whitehaven.

Captain Jones looked around as his men ran back towards the guardhouse and their waiting craft. In the improving light he could see Lieutenant Meijer preparing the rowing boat ready to leave. Behind him at the Old Quay Lieutenant Wallingford appeared almost ready to return to the USS *Ranger*. In the harbour itself the *Thompson* seemed to be well lit. It looked as if a calling card had been left that might make the British think about their own priorities, attacking American ports or protecting their own ports.

Captain John Paul Jones was well pleased with events.

Chapter 10
Warning the Whitehaven Residents

It was chaos. The largest ship in the harbour *Thompson* was now well and truly in flames. The Americans had one boat pushing off from the Old Quay and on the other side of the harbour a second boat appeared to be ready to leave. There was little that the few Whitehaven residents who were on the quay could do.

However, close by on Marlborough Street a sailor was knocking on the front doors of the houses to warn the occupiers of the dangers. David Freeman knocked as hard as he possibly could on a front door. Then moved towards the next house. As he moved between the houses he was calling very loudly, 'Fire, fire.' Then he returned to the first door and knocked again.

So David was developing a good sequence. Knock at a door, move towards the next house and call loudly, knock on the second house, call loudly and back to knock again at the earlier house.

Slowly at first but increasingly quickly the inhabitants of that street were stumbling out on to their street. They were becoming aware of the problem, but totally unaware of the incredible circumstances that had led to the fires.

As the residents had begun to emerge from their houses, David started to organise rather than knock on doors himself.

'Knock on other doors,' he called.

'Go to the end of the street and knock on some doors,' he directed.

At first the Marlborough Street residents did what was asked of them. Then a few began to wonder who was doing all the shouting and organising in their road. The sailor making all the commands was not a resident of Whitehaven.

'Which boat are you from?' One resident called out.

'How did you get to know about the fire? Where were you?' called another.

Within minutes a small group of the residents had

formed a circle around this sailor who seemed so keen to help them.

'None of that matters. We need to protect your houses and the warehouses,' replied David.

'Aye we do that and we're grateful to you lad,' spoke what appeared to be the eldest of the Marlborough Street group. 'You did well.'

After a short pause the white-haired spokesperson, Walter, inquired further. 'How did the fire start? Do you know what happened?

David looked around; this might be a bit difficult to explain. He felt that he would have to tread carefully. 'I saw the fire start on the *Thompson* and it looked as if the *Saltham* might catch light.' He paused then added, 'so I came to warn you in case any sparks reached your houses and the warehouses.'

'Do you know how the fire started,' someone called out.

'Your town was raided.'

'Raided? Who by? Why?' The questions were now coming from all directions and David was beginning to feel somewhat threatened.

'It was an American raid.'

'American?' was uttered by more than one person. 'American?' 'Are you sure about that?'

'American it was. I was forced to sail with them and left their company as quickly as I could.'

As David indicated that he had been one of the raiding party; the crowd surrounding him seemed to become more aggressive and threatening.

'Have you done this to our town?'

'No, I came to warn you, not set light to your town.'

Still there were mutterings from the increasing crowd.

'Stop.' Again it was Walter who took the lead role. 'Did you go on any of the boats in the harbour?'

'No. I just looked out for any opportunity to get away from the raiders so that I could stay in England. Then once away I wanted to warn you because you seemed to be nearest to the danger from the fires.'

There was still some muttering. However that was stopped short by the interruption from Walter. 'We perhaps owe this young man for giving us a warning.'

The mutterings became less frequent and were quieter as well.

'We're thankful to you young man,' added Walter.

With that, the attention of the crowd was diverted to the street and the houses. Some of the men started to organise buckets of water in case the houses needed to be doused to stop any flames spreading. A few of the men and women moved down to the quay to check the warehouses. There was very little gap between the warehouses and the harbour. The buildings had been planned to be close by to make the loading and unloading of the various cargoes that much easier.

As the growing crowd diverted to the harbour or to checking the property in Marlborough Street only Walter and David were left standing in the centre of the road with some women moving in and out of their houses.

Two women approached David and Walter, 'Thank you for the warning,' one of them said. The other just smiled and nodded her agreement. Immediately they turned and went back to checking their homes.

Walter looked from the women and back to David. 'You took a bit risk today lad. First in escaping from the American ship and then as well in keeping my neighbours safe.'

'I think I owe you for keeping me safe,' responded David.

'Perhaps so. You might still need to be very careful. Not everyone is going to thank you for your help. Some may question your role in the attack rather than being grateful for all the help you have given.'

Walter and David walked to the nearby harbour. All the signs were that the warehouses were safe, at least for the time being. There were still large flames and smoke coming off of the *Thompson*. The other ships in the harbour seemed to be safe, at least for the moment.

'If the other ships and the warehouses remain untouched that will help your cause David,' stated Walter.

David stood by the side of the harbour and looked at each ship as best as he was able to do. He was pleased to see that only the *Thompson* was in flames. And the warehouses did look safe for the moment. He realised that Walter was right; if all but the *Thompson* stayed safe his own safety would be much improved. At that moment three of the previously angry crowd headed towards Walter and David. Each of the men had a large hammer. They stopped directly in front of the pair.

'Well done, to you lad,' said the tallest of the trio, while placing his hammer on the ground.

'You've helped to save a good part of the town.'

'We will remember your quick thinking and help,' added another of the group.

The trio then turned and headed back into Marlborough Street.

For the first time in days David felt much better. Events seemed to have worked well. It looked like it was not the disaster he had worried about.

Chapter 11
Putting out the fires

While there was a commotion in the town, it was being organised for the two boats from the USS *Ranger* to be rowed back to sea and away from the town. First, the nearer of the two boats captained by Lieutenant Samuel Wallingford was made ready.

'Ready to move as quickly as possible,' called Midshipman Ben Hill softly.

'Do we have everyone?' asked Lieutenant Samuel Wallingford.

'Gap here,' indicated a sailor in mid-boat.

'Who was there coming out?'

'Not sure sir,' came the reply to the lieutenant's question.

'Who is missing?'

'I think it may be Freeman, sir.'

By now the Lieutenant was getting annoyed. He

could not afford to keep the boat in harbour for too long, but he didn't want to lose anyone either

'Is Freeman here?' he enquired.

As there was no response he changed the question. 'Has anyone seen Freeman?' Again there was no response.

After a short thoughtful pause Lieutenant Wallingford gave the command. 'Alright Midshipman we'll move off. Freeman may have got caught up with the other crew. We can't sit here any longer.'

With all the commotion on the quay the boat was able to slip away and head towards the other side of the harbour. From there the two boats would be able to head back to the *Ranger*. However, that return trip was without David Freeman. He was not on either boat and had made himself scarce in the town as well.

The nearest boat had been close to all the activity but the Whitehaven residents were too occupied with ensuring their own safety and the protection of their houses. Then there was the *Thompson* that needed to be saved. There was no time and very few weapons to engage with the Americans.

What there was in Whitehaven were well-organised

fire services. The town had two fire engines, although in reality they were no more than pumps with an attached hosepipe. They did not include a tank for storing water. So the water had to be extracted from the harbour and then pumped on to the boats. The fact that the tide was rising was a good help to the two fire crews.

Since the previous century when there had been the devastating Great Fire of London many English towns had developed effective fire equipment. These were being developed constantly. Indeed at about this time too in Scotland, James Watt was working on his revolutionary steam-driven fire engines. So the firefighting equipment was about to be developed further still.

The emphasis upon firefighting had been established and now was put into action in Whitehaven. The fire engines had been rushed down to the harbour. There the firefighters first established that the warehouses were safe.

'Are all the warehouses saved?' called one of the firemen.

'We're checking each door,' came the reply.

The doors provided a very good indication whether there was any heat developing that might suggest that the fire was a threat.

'They all seem to be alright,' came the confirmation.

'Good, but keep checking.'

Then the fire in the harbour seemed to be limited to the *Thompson*. The task for the firemen was beginning to look manageable. All of this activity had made the departure from the quay much easier for the Americans.

'We need to stop the fire before it reaches the rigging,' called one of the firemen, as he tried to reach the *Thompson*. Once on board he was able to direct the operations.

Almost immediately, under those instructions the firemen were able to start pumping water onto the *Thompson*. At first the men concentrated upon keeping the rigging wet and pumping water around the base of the main mast. Then, as the fire seemed to lessen and the rigging appeared secure, they just tried to dampen down all the smouldering fires.

As well as attending to the *Thompson* one of the firemen together with some of the Marlborough Street men were able to scout round and check on the other craft. All the ships seemed to be untouched by the fires on the *Thompson*. Nevertheless the men carefully went back and checked every ship in detail.

'This ship is completely clear,' one of the men reported to the fireman. All the checks were important. Smouldering wood could turn into a fire with a slight puff of wind together with some heat from the *Thompson* fire.

Again and repeatedly the reports gave the all clear for the ships in the harbour. Then came the important shout.

'The *Saltham* appears to be alright,' called a fireman from that ship. Apparently the torches thrown onto that ship had largely failed. It was the ship that had been most in danger after the *Thompson*. And with the rigging on the *Thompson* now wet and cold the chance of any fire spreading from one craft to the other had largely disappeared.

While the fires were being fought other townsfolk were sending out messengers to warn the militia in Penrith and to get warnings to ports north and south of Whitehaven.

With all the activity around the Old Quay the first of the American boats had been able to escape danger. The other boat with Captain John Paul Jones on board and Lieutenant Meijer in charge was also ready to depart. Again it was Jake Smith who was at the front of the boat to give any guidance that was needed. He was probably going to have to give less guidance this time because with the ever-increasing light it was easier for the Lieutenant to see where he was guiding the boat.

'Are we ready to move off?' asked the Captain.

'Yes sir,' replied the lieutenant as he also gave the order to cast off.

The Americans had taken three prisoners and two of those were on board the Captain's boat. One had been a recent recruit to the *Saltham*. The other had more unfortunately just gone down to the pier to fish when the returning Americans had surrounded him. George Jefferson had previously been the master of the *Isaac* and the *Barbary*; he was now a prisoner and off to sea again with the USS *Ranger*.

The boat turned to head out towards the harbour entrance and then to sea. The timing was perfect as almost immediately they met up with Lieutenant Wallingford's boat.

'We'll keep a distance apart,' called the Captain looking at Lieutenant Meijer, but also informing Lieutenant Wallingford.

'We don't want to be a target for any guns that they might be able to use.'

With that command the two boats began to move towards the harbour entrance. They were on their way, rowing back to the USS *Ranger*.

Chapter 12
Firing at the American boats

Captain Jones and Lieutenant Meijer had just organised the boat to be pushed away from its mooring when rescuers reached the guardhouse.

'What happened here?' The rescuers asked of the guards.

'We were attacked by a large group; we had no chance,' replied the sergeant.

'Who were they?'

'They could be pirates, but one spoke with a Scottish accent, and there were some Americans too.'

'Well, whoever they are, they seem to be getting away.'

The sergeant responded quickly, 'They spiked the guns but we need to check them. There might be one or two that are not spiked fully.' The sergeant had decided that trying to get a gun to fire would be better than answering questions about how they were all tied up.

While this conversation was taking place others including the sergeant were untying the guards.

'Come on then,' called the sergeant, then added 'bring a hammer and a crowbar; we'll see what we can do.'

'This is where the guns are spiked,' the sergeant told the other guards and the rescuers. 'We need to look for a gun where the spike is not fully hammered home. We might be able to prise it out and use the gun.'

'One here, sergeant.'

'Good. Let's see if we can get the spike out. If we can get under the head of the spike we might lever it out.'

'Another one here, sergeant.'

'Good, this one should come out.'

'Get the crowbar under the head. That's it and tap and push. Yes.'

'Load this gun and I'll try the next spike. This one is easier, it's definitely coming out. Good man, this gun as well.'

A guard came running towards the two guns being loaded. 'I don't think there are any more that we can get to work quickly.'

'Alright, you help with this second gun. First gun fire when you are ready and the second join in to fire. Check the distance. Watch your elevation. They're going to be a hard target to hit. Come on. Fire and fire.'

'BOOM.'

The sound of a 32-pounder being fired was a major surprise for everyone in the escaping boats. Looking back it appeared that one of the spiked guns must have been repaired.

'BOOM.'

The second shot came too quickly after the first firing to be from the same gun. So there must be two 32-pounders that were now back working and able to fire at the Americans.

'Row harder now,' called the Captain. 'Carry on, Lieutenant,' he added as he remembered who was in charge of the boat.

'You men are doing well,' Lieutenant Meijer called

out as he re-established his authority of the boat.

'We need to make sure we offer as small a target as possible. We'll try to create a straight line back to the guns.' Lieutenant Meijer was in full command and creating a very difficult, almost impossible target for the gunners back on the battlements.

Jake was excited by the events, slightly worried by the gunfire, but glad that there were two such experienced leaders on board.

'BOOM.'

Again it was a miss.

'Good, well done lads we're getting away. Pull harder now,' called Lieutenant Meijer.

'BOOM.'

That too was a miss but a better shot than the first one. It was close enough to worry about what might happen next.

Jake wondered just how far out to sea would they have to be before they would be out of range. The first of the two shots had been short, but the second had zoomed over their heads. It was clear they were still in range of the 32-pounders, but perhaps not for very much longer. One more shot and if quick a second shot would be all the gunners would be able to manage.

'You've got the distance gun two and you're in line with their direction,' the sergeant called. 'Gun one you were short, aim for further out this time.'

The sergeant impatiently waited for the guns to be made ready again. He realised that they were running out of time to get a hit on these small boats. Indeed the other boat had moved further away from the one they were aiming at. It was probably too late already to get that one.

'Are you ready?'

'Take care.'

'Fire when you're ready.'

'BOOM.'

'BOOM.'

The gunners were benefitting from having fired twice already and they were beginning to speed up. And from the splashes in the sea they were both closer. But not close enough to hit the boat.

'This time men, you're getting closer with each shot.'

'Load up, ready to fire again, quick.'

'Take a careful aim.'

'This is it,' thought the sergeant. Either they would hit it this time or it was probably too late. 'Fire, fire.'

'BOOM.'

'BOOM.'

Again the guns were fired one straight after the other. The first cannonball hit the water just short of the boat. It was a good aim but not quite good enough. When the second cannonball cascaded into the water there was a loud cheer from the observers and gunners on the battlements. The ball had hit the water right next to the boat and the spray had for a moment covered all sign of the men and the boat. However, it was just a brief illusion. The boat had appeared to have been hit and disappeared from sight. Seconds later the rowing boat reappeared into view. It had been close, very close but just a slight bit short of the boat to do it any real damage.

'We almost had them that time. We'll try one more from each cannon,' the sergeant indicated.

'Fire when you can. Check the elevation, the boats are at the far end of the distance we can reach.'

'BOOM.'

'BOOM.'

This time the cheers came from the very wet crew of the rowing boat. The previous firing had drenched them but now they were a safe distance away from where the cannonball hit the water. They also heard the cheers from the boat in front of them. Lieutenant Wallingford's boat had always been a good distance in front. They had not been a viable target for the 32-pounders. They had just been interested but worried spectators in the race back to the *Ranger*.

Back in the second boat the relieved Lieutenant Meijer was able to congratulate the crew. 'We did well lads. We're out of range now I think. We'll keep up the rate of rowing for a short while longer. Just to be safe.'

However, Captain Jones and the men in the two boats were quite safe. They were out of range of the guns and close to reaching the safety of the USS *Ranger*. Back on the battlements the gunners and others from Whitehaven could only watch as the boats headed back to their ship.

In the days that followed the attack three companies of militia arrived from Penrith. A watch system for guarding the harbour at night was developed and an extra battery of guns was established. It was all too late. Whitehaven had been attacked and the raiders had got away.

When news of this attack reached America there would be delight at the achievement. Captain John Paul Jones and his men had left their mark on England.

Chapter 13
Sailing north to Scotland

All the men received a warm welcome back on board the USS *Ranger*. Captain John Paul Jones immediately suggested, 'A tot of rum,' for everyone returning to the ship as well as to those who had remained behind.

'We'll sail north to Scotland immediately. Head towards Kirkcudbright and the River Dee Mr Simpson, with as much speed as we can muster.'

'Aye sir,' responded Thomas as he recognised the sense of urgency in the Captain's voice.

Captain Jones had in mind that they needed to execute the second part of the trip quickly. Word of the attack on Whitehaven would soon be spread around and so become widely known. It would then become more difficult to mount the surprise attack that he had in mind for Scotland. Without the element of surprise his troops might suffer loses that would be unacceptable. There was too the risk that a number of ships would be sent to the Irish Sea with the express purpose of finding the USS *Ranger*, engaging it in battle and either sinking it or capturing the crew and boat if possible.

'Yes, on our way now Mr Simpson. There is no time to lose.' The wind in the sails indicated that Mr Simpson had already met the Captain's demand. The USS *Ranger* was moving quickly north towards Scotland.

Captain Jones stood for a moment and then indicated, 'I'll just get into some dry clothes.'

However, before leaving the deck he looked back towards Whitehaven. There was smoke rather than flames coming from the harbour. He didn't mind that that was the case. They had achieved what he wanted and what Benjamin Franklin had hoped for. They had had a successful raid on England and a return to the USS *Ranger* without any injuries to his crew. Now he needed to win some more trophies for the men to share. They deserved a reward for facing up to the dangers of an attack so well.

'Lieutenant Wallingford, are all your crew safe and without injury?'

'They are Captain. But, we may have left one sailor behind.'

'How so?'

'He wasn't on the boat when we pushed away from the harbour. There was no time to wait as the town's people were beginning to grow in numbers. And we were already moving when we found out there was a gap on board.'

Captain John Paul paused for a moment then asked, 'Who was it?'

'A David Freeman, sir.'

'Alright, thank you Lieutenant.'

Captain John Paul looked at the men on deck. They had done well he thought. Just one man lost from a difficult attack.

'Do we know anything about what he was doing while we were in Whitehaven?'

'Nothing, sir.'

'Right, see if you can find out anything from your men. You all did really well.'

Jake Smith and the other midshipmen as well as

the lieutenants were still on deck. Some of them were soaked through. John Paul looked across at his officers and felt a tingle of pride in his crew.

'Thank you men. You all did well. It was a difficult and dangerous task but we succeeded. You have my warmest thanks and your nation salutes you.'

Once he had spoken he moved among the men, looking each one in the eye and then shaking hands with each of the officers and midshipmen. As he did so he added a short word of praise.

'You did well,' or 'thank you.'

With some of the men he was able to make a more specific comment about the events.

'You did well at the guardhouse. It was a neat roll away from the door after you opened it for us all to enter,' he said to Jake with a wide smile.

'Don't you agree men?' he added.

There were various cries of 'yes,' and 'aye,' as the men of course agreed with their Captain.

'We might have still more adventures later today when we reach Scotland,' he announced more widely as he looked northwards towards their next point of call.

Finally when the Captain was satisfied that everything was under control he was able to go below deck to get into the dry clothes that he had been looking forward to since arriving back at the USS *Ranger*. The other officers and midshipmen who could be spared also went below deck to dry off.

It was only a matter of minutes before the Captain arrived back on the deck already changed into dry clothes and eager for the next stage in their daring adventures. Before saying a word he walked around the deck, his eagle eye noting that everything was in place and that the USS *Ranger* was moving well through the water.

'So Mr Simpson all seems well. Are we making good time.'

'We are sir and half of the crew are having some food before that rum leaves them stumbling into battle.'

'Good, although I'm hoping we can deal with the Earl of Selkirk without engaging in any battle.'

Captain Jones had discussed his plans with Benjamin Franklin in Paris while the USS *Ranger* was being made ready for battle. Dr Franklin considered it to be a worthwhile project that might be of real benefit to the 13 states.

'But will it work?' Franklin had asked.

John Paul had thought about that question ever since it was asked of him. His plan was a simple one to land on St Mary's Isle, an isle that was actually a peninsula with a narrow strip of land that connected it to near the southern edge of the town of Kirkcudbright. St Mary's Isle was not too far from where John Paul had grown up as a child. It was a short journey but one that could best be made by sea rather than land.

The bold plan quite simply required that they capture the Earl of Selkirk who was a close friend of the King. Then they would take him back to America and demand a ransom for his safe return.

John Paul smiled again at the audacity of his plan. It was a bold move for the lad from Arbigland to consider the capture of Douglas Dunbar, the fourth Earl of Selkirk. As he considered the plan, again his thoughts were brought back to the present.

'Almost there, Captain,' Thomas indicated softly.

'Yes, of course Mr Simpson.'

John Paul checked the position of the ship and its

closeness to St Mary's.

'We'll get as close as we can to the shore then row in the last short distance. We must ensure that we keep in deep water for our speedy departure.

'Yes sir,' uttered Thomas who had already done exactly that. They had talked about this part of the expedition enough times to ensure that Mr Simpson knew exactly what to do. Twelve armed crew were already by the rowing boat.

'Good. We'll go now Mr Simpson.'

'Sir.'

'Let's see what the Earl and the King think about this,' said the Captain directly to Mr Simpson.

Chapter 14
On St Mary's Isle

It was a short safe journey for the USS *Ranger*'s rowing boat to reach St Mary's Isle. On this occasion there was no need to watch out for guns that might be fired at them. Avoiding a few rocks as they neared the shore and the selection of the best place to land were the only tasks needing attention.

As ever, however, John Paul wanted everything to be perfect.

'We'll send two men to check the first few hundred yards Mr Simpson.'

'Sir.' Thomas Simpson had already organised this, so a brief nod from him to the two sailors at the front of the boat was all that was required.

Immediately after the two had departed the rest of the men disembarked. They pulled the boat to safety and secured it to a stout tree near the edge of the water. Also another two men had already been told that they would remain by the boat as guards.

'Thank you Mr Simpson. It seems you were well prepared for our arrival.'

'Yes, I hoped so, sir.'

Their conversation was interrupted by the return of the two scouts. Thomas looked across to the Captain who quite simply nodded. Mr Simpson was being given the authority to receive their report.

'Well,' Mr Simpson said as he looked directly at the two men.

'All quiet sir. It's an easy walk to the very big house and that seems to be peaceful. We just met a few of the ground staff. We told them we were part of a press gang.'

'Good. I imagine that speeded up their movements.'

'It did Sir, I don't think there will be too many staff around when we head back to the house.'

'Indeed not. You two can lead the way. When we reach the mansion I want you and the others stationed around it so we cover all the doors. No one goes in, no one comes out.'

'Sir,' was the general reply.

'Let's go then.'

Thomas looked across at Captain Jones as he finished his instructions. The Captain simply nodded his assent. He was well pleased not only that all the preparations had been made but also that he had the support of such a loyal and competent officer as Thomas Simpson.

The raiding party made its way without hindrance to the mansion. Once they had arrived it was but a few seconds before all the men were in place and the two officers were at what seemed to be the front entrance.

'A good strong knock if you will Mr Simpson.'

'KNOCK, KNOCK.'

'Thank you, Mr Simpson.'

Captain Jones was just beginning to become impatient when finally a servant of the Earl slowly opened the door.

'We wish to see the Earl of Selkirk.'

'I'm sorry sir but the Earl is not home at the moment.'

'Perhaps we might come in and wait for his return,' replied Captain Jones.

'It will be another two weeks before the Earl is back; he is in Edinburgh. Perhaps I should let the

Countess know of your arrival. Who are you sir?'

'Captain John Paul Jones, commander of the USS *Ranger* from the United States.'

'Thank you, if you'll just wait here I'll let the Countess know.'

John Paul considered the information he had been given. If true, then this second part of their mission, the raids on land was not going to achieve its aim. He glanced across at Thomas who had an obvious look of disappointment.

The servant returned and suggested, 'If you will follow me I will escort you to the Countess.'

'Thank you, lead on,' he replied. Thomas remained at the main entrance to the mansion.

The Countess, much younger than Captain Jones imagined, cautiously welcomed him into the main living room.

'You are, sir?' She asked.

'Captain John Paul Jones. My ship is the American sloop-of-war USS *Ranger*. It is just off the isle, milady.'

'And your business here?'

'My business was to meet with your husband the

Earl. Then to take him as hostage and return him with us to the Americas.'

'But this is outrageous. My husband is neither a soldier nor a sailor. And he has no business with the Americas. This is quite outrageous.'

'I understand that milady but he is a friend of the King and the King constantly sends ships to our shores to do much damage to our ports and people. The time has come for us to raid England and make this brief visit to Scotland. The King will, I'm sure, pay the ransom for the safe return of your husband. Your husband is where exactly, milady?'

'Unfortunately for you he is in Edinburgh on business and I do not expect him back for another two weeks. It is, it seems, fortunate for him that he is away,' the Countess said.

'Yes indeed, fortunate for him. Perhaps my men should just search through the property to check that he is not yet returned,' Captain Jones replied.

'That too sir is outrageous. I have told you of his whereabouts. Do you question my word?'

Captain Jones paused briefly, looking intently into the eyes of the Countess.

'I question not your word, milady. My men and I will return to our ship and carry on the fight for our country. I bid you good day.' With that final comment John Paul turned and departed from the living room. He made his way back to the front entrance and there he immediately noted Mr Simpson together with sailors gathered around the main door.

'The Earl is not here, Thomas. We will return to the ship and then back out into the Solway.' John Paul hesitated then added, 'Is there a problem, Mr Simpson?'

'The men were wondering what trophies had been gained from this visit. They have experienced the Royal Navy raiding their homes and they suggest little sympathy is shown to them or their families. We are at war. Are we to be so different when we land in England or Scotland?'

Captain John Paul Jones didn't like it but he could understand the men's disappointment and even anger. 'Right Mr Simpson I shall leave you in charge. The men are to remain outside while you negotiate the collection of some silver plates or other such valuables.'

The Captain turned to the men. 'Mr Simpson will get us some trophies. We will show the people here that Americans can behave more decently than raiding parties from Britain.'

Although the Countess was taken aback by the apparent change of heart, she decided that the best thing to do was to get her servants to collect together some silver plates and a large tea service. She wanted to get these raiders or pirates away from St Mary's Isle. Her concern was for the safety of her children and the protection of the mansion.

When Mr Simpson returned with these spoils, the mood of the men changed. They were well pleased with their trophies and ready to return to the rowing boat and beyond to the USS *Ranger*.

Captain Jones was less happy with the outcome of the visit. He was troubled by the spoils that had been collected and the manner it was obtained from the Countess. The more John Paul thought about it the less happy he became. He decided upon a course of action. When the opportunity presented itself he was determined to buy the tea service and then return it to the Countess on St Mary's Isle.

Chapter 15
Approaching the *Drake*

With all the crew back on board, Captain Jones was ready for what was expected to be their final event of the trip. The first visit to Whitehaven had been successful and had no doubt attracted much attention. The recent visit to St Mary's Isle had not achieved its objective of capturing an important person as a hostage for a substantial ransom, although the sailors had collected some trophies. It too would attract some attention. It would begin to look as though nowhere was safe from attack.

Now, in a third episode, there was to be an attempt at fighting a major sea battle that could have glorious consequences.

'We'll head south now Mr Simpson for a short distance and then west to have a close look at Carrickfergus.'

It was an obvious command but one that had to be

made. It indicated the completion, even if only half successful, of their St Mary's Isle visit and the start of their next adventure. The sloop soon left the Solway Firth and maintained its journey south and west into the Irish Sea.

Carrickfergus was the town where the USS *Ranger* had sailed close to the Royal Navy warship, *Drake*. The Irish town, on the north shore of Belfast Lough, often sheltered Royal Navy vessels. Captain Jones was hopeful that the *Drake* might be found there.

'Mr Simpson we'll fly the ensign until we are up close. Get the men to check all the guns and bring them in behind their port holes I think.'

'Sir,' replied Thomas who was already starting that process.

The men on board the *Ranger* had not been told directly about what was intended. They didn't need to be told. The commands from the Captain could be heard easily enough. Also the men were competent sailors so that they knew which way they were heading. The cleaning of the guns was the final clue. It made the men excited by the prospect although with a slight concern, inevitably, about the outcome.

The men worked quickly and carefully to prepare the guns. It was important to each one of them that everything was in good order. Their own lives were at risk if the guns were not well prepared.

Lieutenant Simpson too wanted everything to be perfect. All the men seemed well prepared and it was at that moment that he spotted a large ship at anchor in the main channel.

'A large ship at anchor, sir,' called out Thomas as he handed the telescope to the Captain.

'It might be what we seek,' replied the Captain handing the glass back to his lieutenant.

Jake and the other midshipmen were excited too. The trip to St Mary's Isle had meant little to them as they were not involved. They had merely waited on board the *Ranger* while the small group of sailors had landed and returned shortly afterwards. Now there was the prospect of a real battle. This time instead of being a battle on land, like at Whitehaven, it looked like being a sea battle against a larger ship that perhaps outgunned them.

So the midshipmen were excited but of course there was also concern about what might happen. This time it was not likely that they would find the sailors asleep like the guards at Whitehaven.

'We will need to use our greater speed and manoeuvrability if we are to win the day here Mr Simpson.'

'Sir, all the men are ready for the tasks they need to perform.'

Thomas Simpson again looked through his telescope. 'They are sending a boat across to us from the *Drake*, sir.'

'Let's see if we can entice them aboard Mr Simpson. Keep the stern facing the *Drake*. I don't want them to see our broadside. Well, not straight away Thomas. Not straight away.' John Paul smiled as he thought about the strategy and the battle to come. 'The *Drake* can certainly see and feel our broadside later on,' he thought.

'I don't think the officer knows what to make of us,' Thomas suggested as the boat was rowed ever closer to the USS *Ranger*. 'He has his telescope on us but he's not sure.'

'Who are you? What ship are you?' came the call from the rowing boat as it came up close to the *Ranger*.

Captain Jones was now able to put on his best Scots accent to fool the officer into thinking the *Ranger* was a British merchantman.

'I'm coming aboard,' called the officer.

'We are short of men already,' replied John Paul. 'There are no press sailors on board here.'

Lieutenant Samuel Wallingford had his marines all ready. This was what they were truly trained for; the marines were expert sharpshooters. Their muskets were loaded and pointing directly at where the British officer and his six men were about to appear on board the *Ranger*.

'Welcome to the USS *Ranger*,' said Captain Jones. 'We are an American sloop-of-war. I am Captain John Paul Jones; news of our attack on Whitehaven may have reached you.'

'News indeed Captain. I think you will have the Royal Navy out hunting for you and the King will probably be getting the hangman prepared to attend to you with a sturdy gibbet.'

'Perhaps so,' suggested Captain Jones. 'But I think we will start with your sword. As you can see, you are well outnumbered and the marines are very accomplished sharpshooters. So your sword as an act of surrender and your men to lay down their arms.'

The two midshipmen, and friends, Jake and Samuel stood on the main deck each with a pistol at the ready. Both were excited to watch the events unfold but hoped that they could be victorious without the need for the pistols. Jake noticed how much more confident his friend Samuel had become since leaving France all those days ago. He hoped that perhaps he too had grown in confidence and usefulness to the Captain.

On deck the British officer handed his sword to Captain Jones and his men followed by placing their weapons upon the deck. There was little else that they could do, as the American sharpshooters surrounded them.

The boom of a gun from the *Drake* was a signal of recall to bring the officer and men back to the ship rather than a start to a battle. But the recall was too late. The British officer and his men had already been escorted down into the hold and away from the battle that was to follow. The rowing boat that they had used to reach the *Ranger* had been cast off. It was too cumbersome to be retained. Speed of movement was going to be a vital asset for the Americans.

Captain Jones realised that the time when those on board the *Drake* would be satisfied with the credentials of the *Ranger* was fast disappearing. The time to do battle was almost upon them.

'Are we ready Mr Simpson?'

'We are Captain, the men are ready; the guns are prepared.'

'Then we must do our best for ourselves and for America.'

Chapter 16
Battling with the *Drake*

The wind and tide were against the boats making a quick exit. It was difficult for them to leave the Lough and sail into the North Channel that runs between Ireland and Scotland. However it was easier for the lighter, quicker more manoeuvrable USS *Ranger*. As it moved out of the Lough it kept to a speed that the *Drake* could just about manage. Captain Jones wanted to encourage the *Drake* out of the harbour and throughout much of the day of April 24th 1778 he did exactly that.

In late afternoon the more favourable wind and tide suggested the time for battle had arrived.

'We'll let the *Drake* close up on us a bit, Mr Simpson.'

'Aye, aye Captain,' replied Thomas.

Jake and Samuel glanced across at each other. Their meaningful glances without any word spoken nevertheless conveyed a great deal. The sea battle that they had envisaged for some weeks was about to occur. They were excited by the prospect of the sea battle, but also slightly afraid that they might not be able to meet the demands to be made upon them.

The Captain looked across at the two young midshipmen, 'You'll do well. You have done so already on this journey. Stay calm and focus on your task.'

Jake and Samuel were again delighted to be spoken to so sympathetically by the Captain. Jake felt that increasingly the Captain trusted him and Samuel.

'Sir,' was nevertheless as much as they could muster by way of a reply.

The *Drake* was now close enough to be within calling distance.

'What ship are you?'

The time for deception was now past. The Captain loudly and proudly proclaimed, 'We are the USS *Ranger*, the American sloop-of-war.'

So with their country of origin revealed, the sea battle was bound to follow.

'Take down the ensign Mr Simpson. We'll have the

stars and stripes if you please.'

'We'll let the *Drake* follow us just for a few more moments then we'll turn and give it a broadside.'

'Aye Captain,' Mr Simpson was pleased to reply.

The *Ranger* had the manoeuvrability and speed to do exactly that. It had been built for war with 18 guns to provide a powerful broadside. In contrast the *Drake* was bigger, heavier and had been built as a merchant ship. It was only the previous year that it had been converted to a warship. Even the 20 four pound guns were old guns that the merchants had installed for protection. Those guns could provide 40 pounds on either side for a broadside attack. The *Ranger* had two guns less but they were 6 pounders so their broadside was stronger than that of the *Drake*. The USS *Ranger* with fewer guns would broadside 54 pounds from either side of the sloop.

Still the *Ranger* was patiently kept in front of the *Drake* and led them both into the North Channel.

'Ready for a broadside Mr Simpson? We'll turn sharply under your order.'

Captain Jones then turned towards Lieutenant Wallingford, 'I want your marines to shoot at the top riggings, masts and sails. Let's see how much damage your expert shooters can inflict on the *Drake*.'

Thomas Simpson gave one last look around the *Ranger* to make sure everything was ready for the battle. He then gave the order.

'Hard about.'

'Ready for a broadside.'

Then a call to the gunner and gunner's mate, 'Fire when ready.'

There was a brief pause while the gunner checked for the best position against the *Drake*, then, 'Fire.'

'BOOM, BOOM.'

The sound was deafening, especially as it was followed immediately by the marines shooting at the top points of mast and sail on the *Drake*. Jake and Samuel followed suit with their pistol shots aimed at the high rigging and sails. Their attempts did not add very much to the efforts of the marines but they felt that they were at least making some contribution to the battle. The noise from the battle was such that there was soon an audience assembled on the shore at Port Patrick.

'Fire.'

'BOOM, BOOM.'

On board the *Drake* there was pandemonium. They had been hit by two broadsides before they were able to fire their guns for the first time. The rear gun when fired was found to be unstable and a real danger to those firing it. The remaining nine guns on that side suffered also. First, they had a tendency to tip forward when fired so that the shot was well short of the target. Then, the slow matches used by the gunners kept going out so there was not a reliable nine-gun broadside when firing. Finally, even after managing a broadside they found that the *Ranger* had a toughened hull that had been built like that for the express purpose of protecting the sailors on board.

In the meantime the *Ranger* had got off its third broadside.

'Fire.'

'BOOM, BOOM.'

The strategy of firing at the rigging, masts, and sails was proving to be highly successful. The *Drake* had started as the slower of the two ships and the less manoeuvrable of the two ships. Added to that the ship now had a reduced capacity as its sails were shattered and made useless under the heavy bombardment from the *Ranger*. The *Drake* was finding it ever more difficult to stay in the battle to any real extent. The hope within the *Drake* had been to get close enough to get grappling irons across and use their superior numbers to attack the *Ranger*.

Captain Jones was aware of being outnumbered and made sure not allow the two boats to get too close to each other. In that objective he succeeded. However, the *Ranger* had not gone unharmed. First, it was a major shock when a musket shot to the head from the *Drake* killed Lieutenant Samuel Wallingford instantly.

Captain Jones was deeply distressed when he heard that his marines' leader and friend had been killed. Then two further marines had been killed when a broadside by the *Drake* had reached their position in the masts. By the end of the battle a further five had been wounded.

On board the *Drake* the casualties were somewhat higher. Five of the sailors had been killed and a further 20 had been seriously wounded. Being wounded at sea in 1778 was not a very safe option. Many sailors died from their wounds on board ship and later when they were in hospital on land. The help given was, of course, limited by the medical knowledge of the time and the lack of detailed attention given to hygiene during treatment.

One of the deaths on board the *Drake* was that of the Captain George Burdon. Earlier, Lieutenant Dobbs had been seriously wounded so that command of the *Drake* had now passed to the master John Walsh.

A few minutes after the death of the Captain it was suggested to the master that the colours should be struck and the vessel should be surrendered to the *Ranger*. The master rapidly assessed the situation. The sails and rigging were in tatters. The *Drake* was very largely immobilised. The battle had gone on for a few minutes more than an hour. It was clear to all that the battle was over. The *Drake* could now do very little to defend itself from the battering it was getting. John Walsh realised that the battle was over.

So great had been the battering that the colours had been shot away. To surrender, the master could no more than wave his hat vigorously and then shout across the water that the *Drake* was surrendering.

'Mr Simpson I think the *Drake* has surrendered. A ceasefire is called for if you please,' ordered Captain Jones.

Jake and Samuel looked at each other and grinned. They were going to be safe. They were also filthy from all the gun smoke that had covered the battle scene. At the sight of each other the smiles turned to laughter. Then quickly they returned to the main deck to provide whatever support Mr Simpson decided upon.

Captain Jones looked across at the very battered *Drake* and then at the *Ranger*. It was very obvious who had been victorious in the North Channel Naval Duel. The warship of the American Navy had left yet another important message for the British to consider.

Chapter 17

Returning to France

Captain Jones scoured the skyline with his telescope. The *Ranger* was very near to land, too near perhaps. There was Ireland to the west, Scotland to the east and England a further distance to the south of the ship. There did not appear to be any large ships near by. Yet it had also been obvious that the officers on board the *Drake* had been aware of their exploits in Whitehaven. So being alone might not last long for the *Ranger*. It was important to get away from the North Channel to a safe haven.

Captain Jones was right to be concerned. The Royal Navy were deploying warships from ports all along the western coastline. The British were determined to capture what they considered to be privateers.

Time was going to be an important factor for the USS *Ranger* and its crew. The *Drake* would be a major trophy for the crew but it was obvious that there would have to be some immediate and quick, repairs to get the ship seaworthy.

'Mr Simpson, there is some major work to be done. The carpenter and some helpers have to get on board the *Drake*. I need to know quickly how soon it will be for the *Drake* to be made ready to sail.'

'Aye, sir.'

'You will need to take the marines on board also. The surrender of the officers and men and the handing over of their arms needs to be completed.'

'Sir.'

As Captain Jones expected, Lieutenant Simpson had already made some arrangements for those tasks to be completed. It took very little time before the carpenters, helpers, and marines to be deployed. Then the master of the *Drake* was escorted across to the *Ranger* where he was able to surrender formally and pass the *Drake* over to the US Navy.

'Are you now in charge of the *Drake*?' Captain Jones enquired.

'I am sir. The Captain George Burdon was killed by a musket ball and Lieutenant Dobbs was seriously wounded by some shrapnel from your broadside and is being attended to by our surgeon.'

'It is an unfortunate aspect of battle that good men get hurt and some die. We too have lost some fine marines and sailors.' As he spoke Captain Jones looked around at the limited damage to the *Ranger*.

Meanwhile Lieutenant Simpson was accepting the arms from the marines and sailors on board the *Drake*. He was surprised to note just how many more men there were on the *Drake*. If the *Drake* had been able to get grappling hooks across to the *Ranger* they might have overwhelmed the Americans.

Now repairs were needed. The important task of getting the *Drake* more seaworthy was in the hands of the skilled carpenter from the *Ranger*. He was able to assess the tasks and began to give jobs to the 35 men from the *Ranger* who had come across to the *Drake*. Sailors from the *Drake* itself were busily working the bilge pumps to reduce the water level in the ship.

'Mr Simpson, we will sail slowly north and west to move away from the scene of the battle. I want us out of the North Channel by nightfall. We will tow the *Drake* until I have your word that she can sail on her own.'

'Sir, one or two days to clear the rubbish and put in new masts and sails. I think that should do it.'

'Good. Yes, good. We won't have much more time than that to get well away from here. There will be Royal Navy warships out hunting for us sooner than we would wish.'

'Aye sir.'

'We will let the *Drake* sailors organise their burials. We must complete those early tomorrow. And the same for our losses – an honourable sea burial by early light tomorrow.'

Jake and Samuel could hardly believe the amount of work being carried out on both of the ships. The noises of sawing and hammering, as well as officers directing with their commands, added to the noise the sailors were making. It all made for another noisy, although certainly less frightening, day. Jake and Samuel too were given tasks to complete, moving from boat to boat with messages, collecting materials, and occasionally completing minor repairs. Neither of them had been prepared for this but it was something to be learned very quickly.

By the time it became dark the two ships were no

longer close to Belfast Lough and they were out of the North Channel. It meant that they were unlikely to be sighted quickly by any searching Royal Navy vessels. In the meantime there was continuing activity on both ships. The carpenter from the *Ranger* remained in overall charge and the carpenter from the *Drake* was also at work to make the *Drake* seaworthy.

The following day too was eventful. First there had been the sea burials. Jake had been surprised by his reaction. He had been moved deeply by the simple service and burial of Lieutenant Wallingford and the two other marines. He had known the lieutenant only briefly and his only real contact had been at Whitehaven. Yet the event brought a tear to his eye. Perhaps that was partly generated by the sheer relief of coming through the battle unscathed himself. As he looked across at his friend Samuel he noted he too was wiping his eye and cheek, a tear from him too.

'Are you alright, Samuel?' asked Jake after the burial.

'Yes, I think it was just because it was all so solemn,' answered Samuel. Although Samuel had expressed fears earlier in the journey he now seemed to have become a more mature and competent midshipman.

Jake hoped that he too had grown in stature during this incredible month of April 1778. 'It was solemn, Samuel, it was solemn indeed.'

'But now it's back to repair jobs Jake.'

Off went the two midshipmen to continue with their chores. Even as they did so there was a commotion as the *Ranger* detained a small fishing boat.

'We'll send some of the Irish crew from the *Drake* back home Mr Simpson,' called the Captain. 'It will be good to reduce the numbers on board the *Drake*.'

'It will sir,' replied Thomas. 'Reducing the numbers on the *Drake* will be very useful.'

Lieutenant Simpson immediately arranged for the transfer of some of the Irish crew. Even the removal of a few sailors made the task of supervising the remaining prisoners so much easier.

During all this time of repair, burial, and transfer of sailors the *Ranger* and *Drake* were making slow but steady progress around the northern coast of Ireland. They were heading steadily out into the Atlantic Ocean and then southwards down the west coast of Ireland. It was a good move.

The Royal Navy was hunting for the *Ranger* in the Irish Sea, and using up valuable time. Meanwhile the *Ranger* was making its escape on the other side of Ireland. Captain Jones only needed to get a few hours start on the chasers to be able to escape their grasp. That was exactly what he was doing.

Once the repairs had been completed Lieutenant Simpson was given charge of the *Drake*. The ship was a valuable prize and John Paul Jones wanted to make sure that it was captained by a sailor that he valued.

Now they were heading south towards France. John Paul wanted to return to Brest then get news of his conquests to Benjamin Franklin, although it was likely that such news would somehow have arrived in France before they did. Once the news had reached London it would soon make its way to Paris.

Jake too was looking forward to returning to France. It would mean safety, at least for a while. He and Samuel had survived perils at Whitehaven, St Mary's Isle, and Belfast.

'I think we are out of the war for a while,' he suggested to Samuel.

'Yes, as long as we can get to France safely.'

'I think we will Samuel and we have left an important lesson for the British. They will have to strengthen every port, harbour, and bay in the country.'

'You're right, Jake, they won't know what we're going to do next. So they will have to protect as many places as they can.'

'Perhaps they will have less time and ships to be raiding the ports of America,' replied Jake as he smiled across at Samuel.

ACKNOWLEDGMENTS

There are numerous accounts of the life of John Paul Jones. They provided me with the basis from which my story could be written. Within the source accounts there are variations as to events that might or might not have occurred. However, the raids upon Whitehaven and St Mary's Isle and the battle with the *Drake* in Belfast Lough are inevitably recorded in those accounts. As is the important battle off Flamborough Head, although that event is not part of the story told here.

Of course my story is a fictional account of the three events. Clearly I have no knowledge of conversations that took place and some characters have been added for literary purposes.

The birthplace of John Paul Jones on the Arbigland Estate south of Dumfries has numerous artefacts. I was fortunate to have my many questions answered by the knowledgeable Sandy Roydes when I visited the site. The museum guide

In Harm's Way by David Lockwood provides a basic account of John Paul's story. Somewhat more detailed is *The Pirate Patriot* by Armstrong Sperry.

Captain Jones's Irish Sea Cruize by David Bradbury is a very detailed account of the three events in April 1778. It is a text written by a 'specialist in writing history from contemporary, primary sources'. The newspaper *The Cumberland Chronicle* is a major source for that very useful book.

Of course there is a wealth of other books, many written in the USA of this very special American patriot with a Scottish background. A visit to the Internet reveals the extent of those texts. The Internet inevitably does more. There are many sites dedicated to John Paul Jones that provide part of the story of this remarkable man.